MISS SUZY

40TH ANNIVERSARY EDITION

BY MIRIAM YOUNG
PICTURES BY ARNOLD LOBEL

PURPLE HOUSE PRESS KENTUCKY

ISBN 1-930900-28-7   LCCN 2004101605
Printed in China   2 3 4 5 6 7 8 9 10
www.PurpleHousePress.com

Miss Suzy was a little gray squirrel who lived all by herself in the tip, tip, top of a tall oak tree. She liked to cook, she liked to clean, and she liked to sing while she worked.

Every morning Miss Suzy made herself a bowl of acorn pudding, and as she stirred it around she sang:

Oh, I love to cook, I love to bake,
I guess I'll make an acorn cake.

After that she swept the crumbs from her moss carpet with a little broom she'd made from maple twigs. Then she dusted her firefly lamps and rinsed her acorn cups and put her whole house in order.

At night Miss Suzy climbed into her bed and looked through the topmost branches at the sky. She saw a million stars. And the wind blew gently and rocked her to sleep. It was very peaceful.

But one day a band of red squirrels came jumping and chattering to the foot of the tree where Miss Suzy lived. They were quarrelsome fellows and liked fighting so much, they even fought among themselves.

Miss Suzy did not see them because she was in her kitchen. And she did not hear them because she was singing:

> I love my house, oh, yes-sir-ee,
> My own little house in my own oak tree.

She was just putting her cake in the oven, when she looked up and saw a lot of strangers in her doorway. One, two, three, she counted, and one, two, three more – six red squirrels.

They chased her out of her little house. They broke
her broom and threw out her acorn cups. Then they
ate up her whole winter's supply of nuts.

Poor Miss Suzy! She didn't know where to go. And
while she stood wondering what to do, it began to rain.
She scampered up the nearest tree. It was a maple
standing beside an old, old house. She ran out on a
branch and dropped to the roof. The rain came down
hard, and her fur was all wet. Shivering and cold, Miss
Suzy scrambled down the chimney of the old, old house
and out of a hole in the chimney and into the attic.

There in the dusty, quiet attic she saw a beautiful dollhouse. It was big enough for a whole family of dolls. She knocked at the door. There was no answer, so she peeped inside.

"My, what a lovely house!" thought Miss Suzy. "It is fit for a queen. But it needs a good housekeeper, so it is just the place for me."

The flowered carpets were covered with dust, and cobwebs clung to the gold chandeliers. There was dust on the black iron stove in the kitchen and on the little piano in the parlor. There was even dust on the china closet in the dining room and a spider web on the dishes inside.

"When it is cleaned, it will be a good house for the winter," said Miss Suzy to herself. "But what a shame there is no one to share it with me. It is so big!"

She cleaned the whole first floor. Then she went upstairs and cleaned the bedrooms. Then she climbed into a four-poster bed and fell asleep.

The next morning Miss Suzy was hungry, and she left the dollhouse to go looking for nuts or seeds. On her way to the attic window Miss Suzy saw a box.

"Just the thing to keep my nuts and seeds in!" she thought, and opened it up. Well, what do you think she saw inside? A band of toy soldiers. They had been sleeping there for years.

"Thanks for setting us free," said the captain. "And now I need a place for us to live."

"Oh, do come stay with me," invited Miss Suzy.

So the toy soldiers marched into the big dollhouse, and Miss Suzy took care of them like a mother. She cooked their meals in the little kitchen and served them in the dining room. At night she told them stories and tucked them into the four-poster beds. The soldiers were very happy. And most of the time Miss Suzy was happy, too. But not always.

Sometimes she looked at the flowered carpets and the real china dishes and the gold chandelier and she sighed, thinking of her plain moss carpet and her fire-fly lamps and her acorn cups.

One night in spring, instead of telling the soldiers a story, she told them about her old home in the oak tree. Then she told them how the red squirrels had come and chased her away, and a tear rolled down her furry cheek.

Late that night the captain woke his men and gave them their orders. There were only five of them, but they were very brave, and their hearts were full of love. After all, Miss Suzy had cared for them all winter.

They marched up to the oak tree and scaled its trunk.

The red squirrels were, as usual, fighting among themselves. They were making so much noise that they did not hear the soldiers until it was too late.

"This is Miss Suzy's house," said the captain, drawing his sword. "Will you go peaceably, or must we fight?"

The red squirrels looked at the soldiers with their shining swords and brave faces, and one by one they scurried, head first, down the tree.

"And don't come back!" shouted the captain.

Miss Suzy was overjoyed when she heard she could move back into the tall oak tree. She thanked the toy soldiers and made them promise to come for dinner once every week. Then the soldiers waved good-bye and marched off through the forest, singing merrily.

Miss Suzy had to work hard to make her old home as neat and cozy as it had been before, but she didn't mind. She made a new moss carpet and a new broom and gathered fresh acorns for cups and caught two fireflies for her lamps. At last she had everything in order.

That night, when she went to bed, she was very tired. But she looked through the branches and she could see a million stars. The wind blew gently and rocked the tree like a cradle. It was very peaceful, and Miss Suzy was very happy once more.